READALOUD
Stories

Then the goblin spoke for the first time. "You only get one wish."

"Oh," said Rosie. "Well, for one thing, I wish you'd clear this mess up. I don't know what Mum will say if . . . "

Her voice faded away into silence. It was magic! It *must* have been magic. All the things on the kitchen floor flew back on to the shelves.

READALOUD
Stories

John Cunliffe
Elizabeth Lindsay
Joan Stimson

Illustrated by David Farris

Hippo Books
Scholastic Publications Limited
London

Scholastic Publications Ltd,
10 Earlham Street, London WC2H 9RX, UK

Scholastic Inc,
730 Broadway, New York, NY 10003, USA

Scholastic Tab Publications Ltd,
123 Newkirk Road, Richmond Hill,
Ontario L4C 3G5, Canada

Ashton Scholastic Pty Ltd,
P O Box 579, Gosford, New South Wales,
Australia

Ashton Scholastic Ltd,
165 Marua Road, Panmure, Auckland 6,
New Zealand

Published in this collection by
Scholastic Publications Ltd, 1990

ISBN 0 590 76303 2

Made and printed by Cox and Wyman Ltd,
Reading, Berks

Typeset in Baskerville by COLLAGE (Design in Print)
Longfield Hill, Kent

10 9 8 7 6 5 4 3 2 1

CONTENTS

1

ROSIE'S GOBLIN

John Cunliffe

"You only get one wish," said the goblin.

"Oh," said Rosie.

Now what do you think Rosie was doing with a goblin in the kitchen at number 23 Hopkins Terrace, Birmingham? Well you might ask. Birmingham is no place for goblins at the best of times, but to choose to appear before breakfast on a wet Bank Holiday, with the shops closed, and Mum in bed with a headache, seemed a bit selfish, Rosie thought, and very ungoblinish. Besides, he'd made such a mess.

Rosie had done the washing up, and swept the floor, and now she had just started putting yesterday's shopping away. (It was that sort of

house.) Mum had bought some of those weird foreign fruit that they have in supermarkets these days — Rosie had no idea what they were called, but she thought she'd have a taste of one. It had a lovely smell, and a pretty skin, with wrinkly patterns all over it, and Mum would never miss just one. So she got the knife out of the drawer and cut one in half.

Then all pandemonium was let loose in that small kitchen! There was a tight little ball curled up in the middle of the fruit, and Rosie thought it was a nut or stone of some kind, at first. But, when she gave it a poke with her finger, it suddenly unrolled itself into a very small goblin, just like the ones in the garden, but without a red cap. It stared at Rosie with winking bright sparky eyes, unfolded its arms and legs, then ran for the open cupboard.

"Come back!" shouted Rosie.

The goblin took no notice. It jumped into the cupboard, and scrambled behind a pile of tins of soup and baked beans, to hide from Rosie. She began taking out cans to uncover its hiding place. She had never seen a goblin before, not in real life, and she was determined to get a good look at this one while she had the chance. But the goblin was just as determined not to be seen, and it dug its way into a new hiding place behind the carrots and potatoes.

"Come out, you little monster," hissed Rosie, not daring to shout for fear of bringing her mother downstairs in a flaring temper because of her headache. But the little creature did not mean to come out. It began throwing things at Rosie, to put her off. It pelted her with potatoes and carrots and onions. It was a good shot too! The kitchen floor was soon littered with vegetables.

"Ooooooh, stop, stop!" screeched Rosie. "I've just put all those away. You'll have Mum down and then we'll both be for it."

The goblin pushed a bag of sugar off another shelf. The sugar swooshed down, like a waterfall, and drifted on to the floor. What a mess! How would Rosie ever get it cleaned up in time?

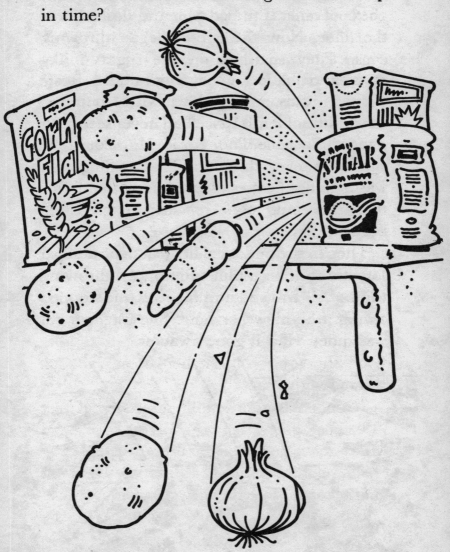

She ran for the dustpan, and began sweeping up the sugar. Her elbow caught a bottle of milk. It tipped over and sloshed over the floor. Now the goblin began throwing eggs. They smashed on the sugary-milky mess, and made a gooey egg-puddle. Rosie slipped in this, and sat down with a bump in the middle of it all. Rosie had never seen such a mess in her life. Poor Rosie! How could she ever clean everything up? That awful goblin was making the mess worse and worse, faster than she could hope to clean it up. Rosie began to cry.

Then in the middle of her tears, she noticed something. The goblin had stopped throwing things. All was still and quiet. Rosie stopped crying. She blew her nose. She listened. All was quiet. Had it gone away?

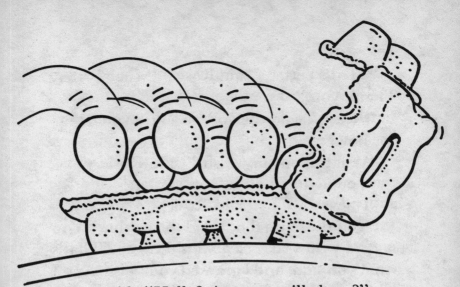

She said, "Hello? Are you still there?"

Then the goblin spoke for the first time. "You only get one wish."

"Oh," said Rosie. "Well, for one thing, I wish you'd clear this mess up. I don't know what Mum will say if . . . "

Her voice faded away into silence. It was magic! It *must* have been magic! All the things on the kitchen floor flew back on to the shelves. Even the eggs went back into their shells, and arranged themselves in neat rows in the egg-trays. In a trice, the floor was as clean and tidy as it was just when Rosie had finished sweeping it. All was in its place in the cupboard.

"That's better," said Rosie. "Much better. Thank you."

"Please," said the goblin. "Will you let me go, now?"

"What about my wish?" said Rosie.

"You've just had it."

"I never . . . " said Rosie.

"You did. You did," said the goblin. "You said, 'I wish you'd clear this mess up.' That's what you said, and I granted your wish. And I told you. You only get one."

"Ooooooh!" said Rosie. "That's a cheat. It wasn't a *proper* wish. There are thousands of things I could really wish for."

Rosie looked as if she was going to cry again.

"Tell you what," said the goblin.

"What?"

"I could give you a present," said the goblin. "The rules don't say anything about presents. *One wish* they say, that's for sure. But presents. They don't say a word about them. And a present isn't a wish, is it?"

"No," said Rosie. "Can I tell you what kind of present I'd like?" said Rosie.

"No no no no!" shouted the goblin. "That would make it a wish. You'll be having me thrown out of the union, and then where would I be? Oh, tut, tut, child. Now hush a minute and let me think . . . I know what you'd like. I'll magic your shoes."

"*My shoes?*"

"Hummmm, yes. If I can recall the spell.
Hush, now. It goes something like this . . . "

Rosie took her shoes off and put them in the
middle of the kitchen floor. She thought the
magic would work better like that. After all,
you take them off to polish them. And she
didn't want the magic to get into her feet. The

goblin muttered to himself in some words that Rosie had never heard before. He was so long about it that Rosie made herself a pot of tea while she was waiting. She was just starting her second cup, when there was a bright flash, and her shoes lit up with a dazzling blue light. The light went out, and the goblin said, "Go on . . . try them."

"What will they do?" said Rosie.

"You'll see," said the goblin, grinning.

Rosie put her shoes on. Nothing happened.

"Well?" she said. "They don't seem like magic to me. They feel just the same."

"Walk," said the goblin.

Rosie walked. She walked across the kitchen.

"So what?" said Rosie. "What's magic about that?"

"Keep going," said the goblin. "In a straight line."

"I'll crash into the wall," said Rosie.

"You won't," said the goblin.

"You're daft," said Rosie.

But she walked. She walked slowly, ready to snub her nose against the wall. Magic or no magic, she meant to do it gently. She didn't want a bleeding nose, and another mess to clean up.

"Go on," said the goblin. "Give it a try."

Rosie walked forward, up to the wall. But she didn't stop, and she didn't crash into the wall, she went *up* the wall.

"Keep going," said the goblin.

18

Rosie went up the wall, and across the ceiling, down the other wall, and back on to the kitchen floor.

"Wow!" said Rosie. "It's great!"

"Told you," said the goblin.

"Will it work outside?" said Rosie.

"Anywhere," said the goblin.

"Wow!" said Rosie. "*Thanks*!"

19

"Let me go, now," said the goblin. "I kept my promise."

"All right," said Rosie.

She opened the kitchen door. The goblin jumped down from the cupboard, ran across the kitchen, out of the door, across the garden, and was gone. Rosie grabbed her raincoat and ran out to see where he went, but there was no sign of him.

Now she was outside, she thought she would try out her magic shoes properly. She walked up the side of the house on to the roof. She walked across the roof of the next-door house, then down the side. Then up the wall of the next house, and so on all up the street. She peeped in at people still asleep in their beds. She saw people brushing their teeth. She made all the dogs bark. She made the cats yowl! Mrs Foster, next door, was up earlier than most. She was sitting over the paper with a cup of tea, when she was amazed to see Rosie walking up the side of the next house!

"Bless me!" she said. "I'm seeing things!"

And she took three aspirins and went back to bed.

It was a good thing that most people were still in bed, it being a Bank Holiday, and a wet one at that. Just think what a fuss there'd have been if more people had seen Rosie!

Then Rosie tried her shoes out on the trees in the gardens. She'd never been any use at climbing trees. Now, she could simply walk up the trunk of a tree, and see the view from the top! No trouble. Oh, and what a view! Could that be Blackpool Tower, far away? The whole town was like a map below her. But the birds didn't like having Rosie in their trees, and set up such a fluttering and squawking that she soon had to come down to the ground again.

It was still raining, and Rosie was getting very wet. Better go home and get dry before Mum got up. It would never do to be found, soaking wet, at the top of a tree. So Rosie went home. She had just one more go across the kitchen ceiling, then she put her magic shoes away, in the cupboard under the stairs, and put her slippers on. How odd it felt, now, *not* being able to walk up walls.

She was only just in time. The bedroom

door opened, and her mother called, "Rosie!"

It was time to put the kettle on for Mum's pot of coffee. And when her mother came downstairs, she looked round the kitchen and said, "Now, my Rosie, what have you been up to?"

Rosie said, "I've been playing with a goblin."

Mother said, "Pull the other leg. It's got bells on it. But I must say you've tidied up nicely. You *are* a good girl when mummy has a headache. All the shopping put away! And the kitchen swept and clean! Lovely! There'll be extra pocket money for that."

It was a lucky thing that Rosie's mother didn't look up at the kitchen ceiling. There was a row of wet footprints right across, from one side to the other. And how could Rosie have explained *that*?

2

NELLIE GOES SHOPPING

Elizabeth Lindsay

It was Saturday. Dad was taking Nellie shopping. Granny May was taking Meg the dog for a walk in the park. There was a jumble of people and dog in the hall, and it got more confusing on the pavement as Meg jumped into the car with Nellie.

"No, Meg," said Nellie. "You're going to the park with Granny May." Meg jumped out again. Granny May had to go back indoors. She'd forgotten Meg's ball. Meg barked, "Woof, woof," which meant "Hurry up."

"No barking, Meg," said Nellie. But Meg wouldn't listen. Going to the park was fun and she wanted to get there.

"Woof, woof, woof, woof, woof," she barked. Nellie put her hands over her ears.

"For goodness sake, do something about that dog," said Dad.

"It's all right. I've found it," said Granny May. She held up the red ball. "Meg had hidden it in her basket." Meg jumped up and Granny May dropped the ball into her mouth for her to carry.

"Thank goodness for that," said Dad, as the barking stopped. "Whatever will the neighbours think?"

"They'll think it's a mad house," said Granny May, laughing. "Come on, Meg."

Nellie watched Meg trot along the pavement beside Granny May, her tail wagging happily.

"I wish I could go to the park too," Nellie said.

"Maybe later," said Dad. "It's shopping first."

Floyd, Nellie's friend from next door, waved to them from his front-room window. Nellie pulled a funny face at him. Floyd pulled one back, and they both laughed.

"Can't play," shouted Nellie. "Going shopping!" Floyd nodded.

"So that's what they're up to," said a curious voice from the roof of Nellie's house.

"I wondered what all the commotion was about. Shopping sounds like fun." The voice belonged to Gertrude the dragon. Gertrude lived in the old shed at the bottom of Nellie's garden.

As Dad started the engine, Gertrude flew from the roof and landed neatly on top of the car. Nellie heard the thud as they were driving off. She looked out of the back window and saw the end of Gertrude's tail swaying behind them. Dad looked in his mirror. He didn't see Gertrude's tail, only the car that was following them.

Gertrude always said, "It's only believers who see us and most people don't." Nellie believed in dragons and so did Meg and Sam, Granny May's black-and-white cat. No one else seemed to. Not Dad, or Granny May, or even Floyd.

Dad drove them to the big car park in the shopping precinct. At the barrier he took his ticket from the machine and the barrier lifted. Nellie heard a squeal of delight from the roof. Dad drove the car into the car park, and the barrier came down behind them. Nellie looked back and was surprised to see Gertrude sitting on the barrier. When the next car reached the barrier the driver took the ticket but the barrier didn't lift.

"Gertrude's weighing it down," said Nellie. "She wants a ride but she's too heavy." The car driver got out and went to fetch the car park attendant. Gertrude got fed up with waiting and jumped down. The barrier went up.

"What's wrong with it?" the attendant asked. "It's working all right." The driver looked confused and got back in the car.

"It wasn't," he said.

Dad and Nellie were already in the lift when a voice said, "Wait for me!"

"Too late!" said Nellie. The lift doors were closing. A golden clawed foot suddenly appeared between the doors and they opened again. Gertrude squashed herself inside. Dad was surprised. There was no one there, yet suddenly the lift seemed very full.

"Why didn't you tell me you were going shopping, Nellie? You know a dragon is partial to a little outing." Nellie didn't say anything in case Dad thought she was talking to herself. He often did when she was talking to Gertrude.

"What are you going to buy? Come on, speak up. I want to know what's what and where we're off to. Are you going to the toy shop? I did enjoy playing with that bouncy ball last time we went." Nellie went hot and cold as she remembered Gertrude and the bouncy ball.

"No," she said. "We're not buying toys, we're getting me some new trainers and an anorak."

"That's right," said Dad. "You can go to the toy department if there's time."

"Goody," said Gertrude.

"No, it's all right, Dad, really," said Nellie.

When they got out of the lift, Dad led the way to the big department store where Nellie was going to try on anoraks and trainers. Nellie, looking over her shoulder, saw Gertrude following along behind.

Inside the store they walked across the ground floor, passing the food store and the ladies' hat department. The children's department was upstairs. Nellie stopped at the sweet counter and was about to ask Dad if she could buy some toffees when she saw Gertrude wearing a long brown wig and trying on a bright green, lacy hat.

"Gertrude!" Nellie gasped. There were startled cries from the customers as Gertrude stood before the mirror in first one pose and then another. They couldn't see the dragon but they could see a floating wig and hat swaying before them.

"Gertrude, take them off, you're causing a sensation!" cried Nellie. But Gertrude couldn't hear above the noisy panic she was surrounded by.

The shop manager advanced with a broom and bravely knocked the hat and wig from Gertrude's head. If only he'd known a dragon was underneath them. Gertrude was furious. Dressing up was fun. She took a deep breath and burnt the broom to a cinder, causing the startled shop manager to drop it. He jumped on the glowing embers which were scorching the carpet.

"Fetch a fire extinguisher!" he shouted. Nellie groaned. Dad stared amazed. He'd never seen anything like it in his life.

"Did you see that? The broom burst into flames," said Dad.

"It was the dragon," said Nellie.

"Extraordinary," said Dad. "If I hadn't seen it I wouldn't have believed it."

"No need to panic, ladies and gentlemen," said the shop manager. "Everything is under control."

Under control, thought Nellie, smiling. Some hopes with Gertrude around.

Gertrude gave up trying on hats. "I'm coming with you, Nellie," she said.

"Why can't you behave yourself?" said Nellie. "It's no fun having you around when you cause so much trouble."

Dad led the way to the escalator, followed by Nellie, who was followed by Gertrude.

"I promise to be good," said Gertrude.

"The trouble with you is that you don't know what good is," said Nellie.

Gertrude did behave on the way up the escalator. But she enjoyed the ride so much she wanted another go. She flew down again over the heads of the people coming up, causing such a draught with her wings that a lady's hat blew off. When she reached the ground floor Gertrude jumped on once again. So did a man in a hurry believing there to be a space. He bumped into Gertrude who gave him a shove with her bottom. The man landed in a heap at the foot of the escalator, wondering why he'd fallen off. Gertrude had three goes on the escalator before hopping off for the last time.

"That was fun," she said. "I wonder where Nellie is?"

Nellie was trying on anoraks. She'd tried on a green one and had on a red one. There was a yellow one and a blue-and-purple one left to try.

"Hello, Nellie, it's me," Gertrude called across the shop. She was balancing with one leg on top of a clothes model wearing a track suit. The model's head was wobbling horribly. Nellie could see that at any moment it was going to break. She shut her eyes. Suddenly there was a terrific crash as the

model collapsed. Gertrude ended up in a
tangle of plastic legs and arms and track suit.

"Goodness," said the shop assistant serving Nellie and Dad. "It's collapsed. I've never known anything like that happen before."

That's because it's never had a dragon standing on its head before, thought Nellie, but she didn't say anything. She watched as Gertrude got up sheepishly from amongst the ruin she had caused.

"Sorry, Nellie," she said. Nellie ignored her.

"I was only showing you how good a dragon is at balancing," she said. "Look at this." Gertrude leaned back on to her tail and wriggled her arms and legs in the air. She looked so funny that Nellie couldn't help laughing.

"Nice to see a smile on your face, Nellie," said Gertrude.

The manager was called by the assistant to look at the broken model. He looked grim. He couldn't understand why it had broken.

"We seem to have a vandal in the shop. One who likes playing tricks," he said. "Keep your eyes peeled. We don't want them to get away."

"Dad, can I have the red anorak?" said Nellie.

"Don't you want to try the others on?" Dad asked.

"No, the red one'll be fine."

When the shop assistant came back, Nellie tried on some blue trainers. They fitted.

"Can I have these, Dad?"

"Don't you want to try any others?" Dad asked. Nellie didn't. She wanted to get out of the shop as fast as possible. Although no one seemed to be able to see Gertrude, she didn't like the thought of her being a vandal. A vandal could be arrested and sent to prison. Why, oh why did Gertrude have to be so naughty?

Dad paid the shop assistant for the anorak and trainers.

"Can we go home now, Dad?" said Nellie.

"Don't you want to go to the toy department?"

"Yes, please," said Gertrude.

Nellie was about to say "No, thank you" when her eye caught sight of a policewoman and a policeman walking between the rows of hanging clothes.

"Quick, Gertrude, quick! Go home," said Nellie. "They might arrest you."

"Me?" said Gertrude. "Arrest me? Whatever for?"

"For being a vandal," said Nellie.

Gertrude was deeply offended. "I am not a vandal, whatever that is. I am a dragon. I'll show them."

She flew into the air and with a graceful glide swooped over the police officers, knocking their hats off, one, two, as she went. She turned and with a flap of her wings disappeared downstairs.

The police officers were not pleased. They picked up their hats and dusted them. Then they took out their notebooks.

"You see?" said the manager. "Someone's playing tricks. It's most upsetting. We're losing business. And the damage. See for yourselves." The police officers began writing.

"Come on, Nellie," said Dad. "Let's go to the toy department." As there was no sign of Gertrude, Nellie didn't protest. She enjoyed looking at the toys and bought a floppy green-and-yellow frog with her pocket money. On the way out of the shop they passed the sweet counter. Nellie remembered she wanted some toffees, but when she looked there wasn't a toffee in sight.

"Well," said the shop assistant to her friend. "It was like the invisible man. The toffees flew through the air into the bag and the bag went out of the shop."

"What? All by itself?"

"All by itself. That's the honest truth. Seeing is believing. It floated out. I've never seen anything like it."

"Didn't you try to grab it?"

"Grab it? Not me. It gave me the fright of my life."

"Let's go home, Dad," said Nellie.

When they got home, Nellie went down the garden to the old garden shed. She opened the door.

"Hello, Nellie," said Gertrude. "You're too late for a toffee." There was an empty carrier bag on the floor and toffee papers were all over the shed.

"Do you know you're wanted by the police?" asked Nellie.

"Me? Whatever for?" asked Gertrude.

"For stealing toffees for one thing. It'll probably be on the news. And look at all this evidence."

"What? You mean the toffee papers?" said Gertrude. "That's easy enough." With a huge breath she sucked up the papers like a vacuum cleaner. Pointing her face towards the door she blew. There was a mighty roar and a stream of flame. Toffee paper ashes floated gently away on the breeze.

"There," said Gertrude. "All gone."

"Really, Gertrude, really, you are the limit," said Nellie.

"Well, what's a few toffees between friends?" said Gertrude.

Nellie let out a huge sigh, shrugged her shoulders and went back indoors. Gertrude lay back on her sacks, licked her lips and smiled a wicked dragon smile.

3

HEGGERTY HAGGERTY
and the
TREASURE HUNT

Elizabeth Lindsay

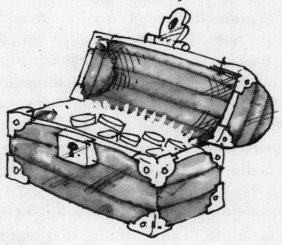

Heggerty Haggerty lives in the cottage at the top of the hill. She has a broomstick called Broomstick and a black cat called Blackcat. As I expect you've already guessed, she's a witch.

One fine spring morning the sun streamed in through the sitting-room window as Broomstick sat down to breakfast. Blackcat lay on the hearthrug washing himself.

"What's this?" asked Broomstick, picking up a large envelope from beside his plate. His name was written in big letters on the front.

"It's for you. You'd better open it and see," said Heggerty Haggerty.

Broomstick held up the envelope to see if he could tell from the outside what was inside, but he couldn't so he opened it. "It's a big piece of paper," he said, shaking it onto the table. "What can it be?"

42

"Don't forget your egg. It'll get cold," said Heggerty Haggerty, smiling behind her teacup.

Broomstick spread the paper out on the table.

"There's a house, a farm, a lane, and a river. It's a map. I wonder who sent it?" he said.

"Blackcat found it on the doormat," said Heggerty Haggerty.

"There's some writing on the back," said Broomstick.

"It says 'Treasure Map'! A treasure map sent to me!" He could hardly believe his eyes.

"All treasure hunters need a good breakfast inside them," said Heggerty Haggerty wisely.

"Bother breakfast," said Broomstick.

Heggerty Haggerty picked up the map. "Breakfast comes first," she said firmly.

"Oh all right," said Broomstick and gobbled up his egg. He wanted to start treasure hunting straight away.

"I've got it," he said, pointing. "This is our house. This is Farmer Giles's farm. This is our lane, and this is our river." He turned the map over. "And this is the clue."

"Read it out then," said Heggerty Haggerty.

" 'Find your way to where the bucket squeaks down, then turn the handle round and round.' That doesn't make sense."

"It does if you think about it," said Heggerty Haggerty. "Where's there a place where the bucket goes down?"

"I don't know."

"Yes, you do. Think."

Broomstick screwed up his face and thought. "Got it!" he cried, and flew out of the door.

"Don't forget the map," called Heggerty Haggerty. "And wait for Blackcat."

Blackcat took the map in his mouth and scampered after him.

Broomstick whizzed down the garden and stopped in front of the old well. It wasn't used any more and usually had a lid on it. Today the lid was leaning against the wall. The wooden bucket that sat on the lid was gone and the rope was dangling down the well.

Broomstick and Blackcat looked over the edge. It was difficult to see down. The roof on the well kept the sunlight out.

"This is the place where the bucket squeaks down, and it is down," said Broomstick. "We've got to turn the handle round and round and pull it up again." He turned the squeaky handle and began to pull the bucket up.

"It's full of water," said Broomstick. And he was just about to pour the water down the well when something at the bottom of the bucket caught his eye.

He put his hand in the water and pulled out a large, flat, shiny stone with writing on it. It was another clue. Broomstick read it out:

"Twirl to the left,
Twirl to the right,
Clap your hands three times
and see the rainbow's flight."

Blackcat looked at the map. He found the well marked by a small black cross. He couldn't see any other black crosses although he looked very hard.

"Come on, Blackcat," said Broomstick.

"Fold up the map. We've both got to do this clue."

They stood side by side. Broomstick counted to three and they began.

"Twirl to the left,
Twirl to the right,
Clap your hands three times
and see the rainbow's flight."

When Broomstick said the last word, there was an orange flash and a rainbow-coloured streamer shot from the top of the well. It flew down the hill towards Farmer Giles's farm. "Follow me" it seemed to be saying.

Broomstick, with Blackcat on his back, flew after the streamer as fast as he could go. They arrived in the farmyard just in time to see the rainbow streamer disappear into the barn.

"That's where the treasure must be," said Broomstick.

They both looked at the map and found the barn straight away. It was marked with a cross.

"Look," said Broomstick. "There's an arrow leading from the well down to the barn."

"That's jolly funny," thought Blackcat. "The cross was by the well before and there wasn't any arrow either."

Blackcat followed Broomstick into the barn. It smelled sweet inside, made so by the piled-up bales of hay. They began searching, Blackcat on the ground while Broomstick flew above the hay and looked inside the big cart. They didn't find any treasure, or the rainbow streamer.

"I can't find anything anywhere," said Broomstick giving up.

"Find what, old chap?" asked Farmer

Giles, who was watching them from the doorway.

"Any treasure," said Broomstick. "We've got a map. We followed the rainbow streamer into the barn which was our clue, and now we've lost it."

"Well, I saw a rainbow streamer fly out through there," said Farmer Giles, pointing to the window at the end of the barn.

"So that's why we can't find it," said Broomstick. "Thanks, Farmer Giles."

They rushed outside.

When they got to the end of the barn they found the rainbow streamer pinned along the barn wall. Someone had painted the next clue on it in big black letters. Broomstick read it out:

"Mark fourteen paces to the apple tree,
Then take six steps to where the beehive be.
The flower pot marks the spot.
Dig down deep until you are hot."

Broomstick called to Farmer Giles. "May I borrow your spade?"

"Help yourself," came the answer.

49

Broomstick grabbed a spade which was leaning against the barn and rushed over to Blackcat. "There's the apple tree," he said. "You pace, Blackcat. I'll count."

Fourteen paces took them nearly to the apple tree.

Blackcat looked at the map. The apple tree and the beehive were clearly marked and between the two was a large black cross. The arrow and the cross on the barn had disappeared!

"Where's the beehive then?" asked Broomstick. There were bees buzzing all round the blossom on the apple tree.

"Watch where the bees go, Blackcat."

The grass was tall and as they peered above it they saw the white top of the beehive on the other side of some brambles.

"Aren't we going to end up in the brambles if we take six steps to where the beehive be?" asked Broomstick. Blackcat shook his head.

Broomstick took six steps towards the beehive and ended up in a patch of earth with an upturned flower pot in the middle. "Blackcat, this is it!" he cried and he moved the flower pot and started to dig.

Broomstick dug and dug, making a deep hole and a huge pile of earth. Blackcat kept checking the map to see if the cross had moved. It hadn't.

Suddenly there was a dull thud as Broomstick's spade hit something hard.

"I've found it!" he cried. "I've found it!" And he uncovered a small box which together they lifted out of the hole and slid on to the grass.

Broomstick was very excited. He struggled with the lock, opened it, and flung back the lid. "Treasure!" he cried. "Golden treasure!"

Broomstick picked up a handful of golden

coins. But they didn't clink like proper money. Then he realised what they were.

"Chocolate money, Blackcat. Chocolate money treasure."

"How nice," sighed Blackcat, as he was rather fond of chocolate.

"Heggerty Haggerty must have made the map," declared Broomstick.

Blackcat thought so too. Magic rainbow streamers and vanishing arrows and crosses were just Heggerty Haggerty's sort of thing.

Farmer Giles lent them his wheelbarrow to carry the treasure home.

Heggerty Haggerty was waiting for them in the living room. "I see you've found the treasure," she said, smiling.

"The best treasure in the whole world," said Broomstick. "Chocolate money."

"Miaow," agreed Blackcat, heading straight for the hearthrug. "The best chocolate money treasure in the whole world." And he curled up for forty winks.

4

THE GIANT NEXT DOOR

Joan Stimson

The Littles couldn't believe their luck. All summer they'd searched for a home in the country. And now they'd found one.

'Bluebells End' was perfect. It had a thatched roof, leaded window panes and a garden bursting with old-fashioned flowers.

"I can't understand why 'Bluebells End' was so cheap," said Mr Little."

"The last people certainly went in a hurry," said Mrs Little. "They've left half their belongings behind."

Jenny Little gazed over the garden wall.

"Look, you can only see one house from here — that huge one on the hill. I wonder who lives there."

"We'll find out soon enough, I expect," said Mrs Little. And they all started to unpack. By evening the Littles had everything organized.

"Phew!" said Mrs Little. "I wouldn't want to do that again in a hurry. I think we could all do with an early night."

For once Jenny didn't argue. She snuggled down in her new room. And promptly fell asleep. Soon afterwards her parents peeped in on her.

"Out for the count," they smiled. But they were wrong.

Just before midnight Jenny woke up with a start. For a moment she didn't know where she was. Then she remembered — and heard the NOISE again!

"Mum! Dad!" she cried. "There's a horrible howling noise and I don't know what it is."

Mr and Mrs Little rushed in to comfort Jenny. Then the noise came again. But they didn't know what it was either. "You don't think 'Bluebells End' is haunted, do you?" whispered Mrs Little.

"Of course not," said Mr Little. "That noise is coming from *outside* the cottage."

Cautiously he peered round Jenny's curtains. A light twinkled on the hill. Then it went out again. As if by magic the howling stopped. The Littles drifted back to sleep.

Next morning the milkman arrived in a blaze of sunshine. Mrs Little was feeling better and went to meet him.

"Welcome to 'Bluebells End'," mumbled Mervyn. Mervyn seemed nervous.

"Thank you," said Mrs Little. "I'm sure we're going to love it here. Just as long as we can get our sleep," she added. "Last night we were woken by the most dreadful howling noise. Did *you* hear it?"

The Littles looked at each other and gulped.

Mervyn shuffled. "I heard nothing," he said. "But that's because I had cotton wool in my ears. You see, the giant often forgets to put out his cat. And then Jumbo kicks up a terrible racket."

"WHAT GIANT?" they all cried together.

Mervyn looked sheepish. "The giant next door," he mumbled. And pointed to the hill. "I'm afraid you're nearest."

"No wonder 'Bluebells End' was so cheap," cried Mrs Little. Then she looked defiant. "But I'm blowed if *we're* moving — just because there's a giant next door!"

Mrs Little put cotton wool at the top of her shopping list and they all tried to forget the giant. The Littles were lucky. For several nights the giant remembered to put out Jumbo.

"It's so *quiet*," said Jenny one morning. "It's hard to believe there's a giant next door."

But Jenny spoke too soon. Half-way through breakfast a terrible burning smell wafted in through the kitchen window. Mrs Little rushed to shut it out. But she was too late.

"Pooh!" said Mrs Little. "Pooh!" said Mr Little. "Pooh!" cried Jenny. "Whatever's that awful smell?"

Just at that moment Percy the postman arrived. He was holding his mail with one hand and his nose with the other.

"Pooh!" cried Percy through the letterbox. "The giant's burnt his sausages again. Every Friday he has a fry-up for breakfast. And every Friday he burns his sausages!"

The Littles were aghast. "No wonder the last people left in a hurry," cried Mrs Little. Then she bristled. "But I'm blowed if *we're* moving — just because there's a giant next door."

Mrs Little put air freshener at the top of her shopping list. She used ten cans every Friday, but you could still smell burnt sausage! And, although the Littles slept with cotton wool in their ears, they often heard Jumbo, howling to be let out.

"Never mind," said Mrs Little one evening. "At least I've got my lovely garden to look out on."

But Mrs Little spoke too soon. Even as she admired the view, a torrent of water gushed down the hill and over the wall. Giant soap suds swamped the sweet peas and the lupins and left a dirty scum.

"Oh no!" cried Mrs Little. Mr Little and Jenny rushed to her side. Just as they arrived, a giant plastic duck crashed against the window. And broke five panes.

There was a dreadful ringing noise in Mrs Little's ears. She was so shaken that at first she didn't realize that it was the telephone. In a daze she picked up the receiver.

"Wit's End," she whispered.

"Pardon?" crackled a voice on the line.

"I'm at my wit's end," whispered Mrs Little. "My garden's swamped with dirty suds. And a giant duck has just broken my kitchen window."

"In that case," said the caller. "I'm too late. This is the Town Safety Officer. I was ringing to warn you that the giant is taking a bath. He usually has one at this time of year. And he *always* leaves the tap running!"

Mrs Little collapsed into a chair.

"*We're moving!*" she said. "I can't stand living next door to a giant a moment longer."

Jenny was sent upstairs to pack. But Jenny had other ideas. She delved under the bed and fished out her Magic Box. This was an old biscuit tin containing her treasures. Jenny rummaged impatiently.

"These should do the trick," she muttered, and stuffed three things into her pocket.

Jenny closed the front door quietly. The Littles were too busy packing to hear her leave. Jenny set off at top speed — up the hill. "We're *not* moving! We're *not* moving!" chanted Jenny in time to her jogging. "We're *not* moving — just because there's a silly old giant next door."

Jenny carried on chanting and jogging. In no time at all she reached the top of the hill. The giant's house was surrounded by a huge wall, but the wall was covered in ivy. Jenny scrambled up one side and down the other.

"SWOOSH!" The grass came right over Jenny's ears. "It's about time the giant mowed his lawn," she muttered.

Jenny waded up to the house. She clambered on to the doorstep and looked up at the great door. For the first time since she left home, Jenny was scared.

She took a deep breath and tapped her pocket. "We're *not* moving," she muttered firmly. And walked along the doorstep.

"That's just like him," cried Jenny suddenly. "The giant hasn't closed his door properly." She squeezed through the gap.

Inside the house it was strangely quiet. And *very* smelly. "Pooh!" cried Jenny. "The giant's been cooking again." Jenny followed the smell — into the giant's kitchen. "WOW!" Jenny looked round the room in amazement. The table legs towered high above her. She would need a ladder to reach the sink or the stove. But Jenny knew just what the giant had been cooking. Because snake-like strands dangled right by her nose. "Ugh! Giant spaghetti!"

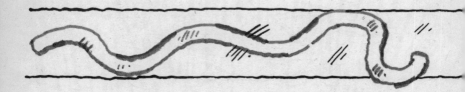

Jenny ducked away from the stove and banged her shin against something hard.

"Ouch!" she cried. "That hurt!" Then Jenny saw what had hurt her. It was the toe of a shoe — the largest shoe she had ever seen!

Jenny scuttled to the other side of the kitchen and looked nervously over her shoulder. Now she could see two enormous shoes. Above them rose two tremendous legs, a massive body and a GIGANTIC head.

Jenny gulped. Suddenly the room filled with a noise like a tractor engine. Jenny jumped a mile. Then she recognized the noise. The giant must have enjoyed his horrid spaghetti. He was fast asleep in his chair. And had just begun to snore.

Jenny took a deep breath. "It's now or never," she muttered. And tapped her pocket.

Jenny tiptoed back across the room. Carefully, very carefully she clambered on to the giant's shoe. Then she caught hold of his trouser leg. And began to pull herself up. At last she reached his knee and stopped for breath.

"Phew!" puffed Jenny. "So far, so good." She began to climb the giant's shirt. Jenny used the buttons as stepping stones and hauled herself on to his shoulder.

"Now!" Jenny whispered to herself and delved into her pocket. She took a giant breath.

First Jenny lifted an old football whistle to her lips. She blew on it with all her strength — right into the giant's ear. Then she wrapped a hankie round her face and cracked open a stink bomb — right under the giant's nose.

Finally Jenny took out a pistol and aimed a jet of water — right between the Giant's eyes!

"Take that, and that, and that!" cried Jenny. She scrambled back down the giant's buttons and trouser leg and leapt on to his shoe.

"WHEEEE!" Just as Jenny was about to jump to safety, the giant reached down and scooped her up. Jenny felt as if she'd left her tummy on the giant's shoe.

'AND WHAT DO YOU THINK YOU'RE DOING?'

roared the giant.

Jenny's knees knocked. There was no point in tapping her empty pocket, but she piped up bravely:

"I'm giving you a taste of your own medicine."

"But I don't need any medicine," roared the giant. He drew his great eyebrows together and glared hard.

Jenny's legs turned to jelly. "Do you mind if I sit down?" she whispered.

Jenny collapsed — right in the palm of the giant's hand.

ʻWHOOOH!ʼ

giggled the giant suddenly.

"That tickles." The giant tried hard to glare at Jenny again. But every time Jenny moved, the giant giggled.

"Now, what — tee — were you — hee — saying about medicine?" he said in a more friendly voice.

Jenny stood tall in the giant's hand. She asked him to carry her over to the window and pointed down to ʻBluebells Endʼ.

"It's all to do with size," began Jenny. "We can't sleep because your giant cat howls so loudly. We can't enjoy the fresh air, because you burn your giant sausages. And our garden is spoilt and our windows broken because you let your giant bath run over."

The giant began to look thoughtful. He carried Jenny carefully to the other side of the kitchen and sat her down on a plate. Then he opened the fridge door. He reached in for a giant sausage and stood it up alongside Jenny. They were just the same size!

"I'm beginning to see," said the giant gently. "A little carelessness goes a long way, when you're a giant. But what can we do about it?"

"Leave things to me," said Jenny brightly.

First Jenny explained how the giant could build a giant cat flap for Jumbo. Then she gave him some cooking tips. The giant licked his lips when he heard the new menues. He was beginning to think he would like to invite Jenny to lunch.

"As for baths," said Jenny finally. The giant looked sheepish. "You don't have enough," went on Jenny. "From now on you should take a bath every day, but *never, ever* leave the bathroom with the tap running!"

By the time Jenny went home that evening, she was firm friends with the giant. She had helped him write

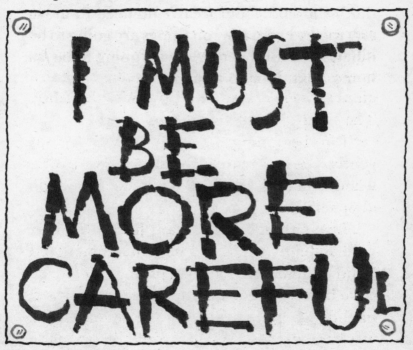

in giant letters on his memo board and the giant said she could visit him whenever she wished.

At 'Bluebells End' Jenny's parents had finished packing. They were out looking for her.

"For a dreadful moment," they said, "we thought you'd gone to see the giant."

Jenny grinned. "That's exactly what I did," she said. "But there's no need to move any more. From now on things are going to be different around here. And it's going to be *fun* living next door to a giant!"

5

NELLIE
and the
SNOWY DAY

Elizabeth Lindsay

Nellie woke up and stretched. It was morning. She could see daylight through the crack in the curtains. Meg lay on the bed watching her. Nellie put her hand on Meg's head and stroked her ears. All of a bustle, Meg jumped off the bed and fetched her blue rubber bone. She jumped up beside Nellie and shook her head.

"I don't want to pull it," said Nellie. "It's too early."

Meg growled and shook her head again. She put the end of the bone in Nellie's hand. Nellie pulled. Meg pulled even harder. Soon the pillows were flying and the bedclothes were all over the floor. Nellie shouted and Meg growled ferociously. Granny May put her head round the door.

"What a row," she said. "Do you have to?"

"Meg thinks she's winning but I am," said Nellie holding up the blue bone. Meg jumped at it and Nellie threw it in the air. Meg dug up a pillow to find it.

"I think you should pull the curtains," said Granny May. "You might have a nice surprise."

"What surprise?" Nellie asked.

But Granny May only said, "Breakfast'll be ready in ten minutes."

Nellie bounced across her bed and pulled back the curtains. Outside the world was covered in white. "It's snowed!" she cried. "It's snowed in the night, Meg."

Nellie ran to the bathroom and had the quickest wash in the world. She scrubbed her teeth until the toothpaste flew. She dashed back to her bedroom and pulled on her clothes.

"It's snowed," she cried. "And it's Saturday. We can play and play all day!"

Meg was excited too and shook her bone vigorously.

After breakfast Nellie pulled on her thick, red, woolly jumper with the green frog on the front.

"My Ferdi Frog jumper'll keep me really warm," she said. Two pairs of socks were pulled onto her feet. Mittens were found and her warm jacket with the furry hood. At last, Nellie pulled on her wellington boots. She was ready.

"I'm going to see if Floyd wants to come to the park," she said. Floyd did want to come. He was tucked up nice and warm and carried a tin tray under his arm.

"What's the tray for?" Nellie asked. They set off down the road with Meg at their heels.

"It's for tobogganing," said Floyd. "My

mum told me how she used to toboggan on a
tray and she gave me this old tin one.''

"Great," said Nellie. "Just great.''

They crunched through the snow as fast as
they could. It was slippery and they clung to
each other to stop themselves from falling
over.

"Meg's all right," said Nellie. "She doesn't seem to slip at all."

"That's because she's got four legs instead of two," said Floyd.

When they got to the park the gates were open and the park keeper was clearing snow from the path. He looked cross and fed up. The children hurried past him. "Remember to keep that dog from digging in the flower beds," he said when he saw Meg.

"I will," said Nellie, wondering if she would know where the flower beds were under the snow.

"Doesn't it look nice?" said Floyd gazing through the trees at the snow on the other side.

"Yes," said Nellie. "It looks wonderful." They left the path and ran into the snow. Meg leapt after them. They picked up handfuls of crispy whiteness and threw snowballs at one another. Meg tried to catch them in her teeth.

"Look at Meg," said Nellie. "She's turning into a snowball herself."

Meg's fur had collected lots of snow. There were great lumps glued to her coat where the fur was long. She didn't seem to mind and began to dig a snow hole.

"Let's toboggan," said Floyd. It took a moment or two to find the tray and they were off, running towards the hill. At the top Floyd put down the tray and sat on it.

"Ready?" shouted Nellie.

"Ready!" said Floyd, holding the sides. Nellie gave him a push. Floyd began to move down the hill going faster and faster. He yelled with delight. By the time he got to the bottom he could hold on no longer. The tray went one way and he went the other, rolling over and over until he came to a stop. He flung his arms in the air and shouted "Fantastic!"

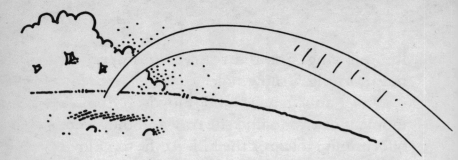

He picked up the tray and began to climb up the hill. Nellie was waiting at the top looking forward to her go.

"That looks fun," said a voice behind her.

Nellie turned round and found Gertrude the dragon. "Can I have a go?" asked the dragon.

"Don't be silly," said Nellie. "You're much too big. Your bottom wouldn't fit on the tray."

"What do you mean?" said Gertrude stiffly. "Are you saying my bottom is fat?"

"No, I'm not," said Nellie. "But it *is* bigger than Floyd's or mine."

"I see," said Gertrude. She turned away.

"Where are you going?"

"To get on with my keep fit. I can take a hint. You think I'm too fat."

"I didn't say anything of the sort," Nellie said.

"You didn't say it in so many words but you said it," replied Gertrude. Her nose went into the air and she marched off.

"Who were you talking to?" Floyd asked when he arrived at the top.

"To Gertrude," said Nellie.

"Oh, come on, Nellie. Why do you keep on with that stuff about a dragon when you know I don't believe it?"

"Just because you don't believe it doesn't mean she doesn't exist," Nellie said and got on the tray.

Floyd gave her a push. She slid down the hill. Gertrude watched from behind a tree.

"It's so bumpy," Nellie cried. "I can't stay on." Nellie, like Floyd, ended up in a heap in the snow. This was Gertrude's chance. She flew from her hiding place down the hill. With a graceful swoop she picked up the tin tray and glided off with it. It was gone before Nellie got to her feet.

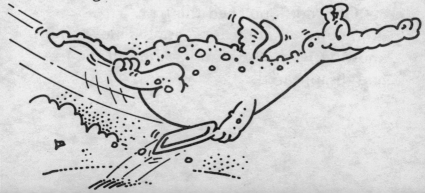

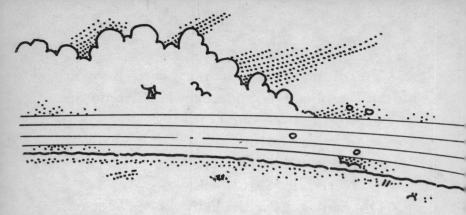

"Where did the tray go?" Nellie asked.

Floyd came slithering down the hill to help look. Nellie didn't notice Gertrude at the top of the hill wriggling her bottom on to the tray. She could only get half of it on at once.

"Oh, botheroo!" she said. "It *is* too small." She pushed forward. "Here I go!"

Meg barked encouragement. Nellie looked up. "So that's where it's gone," she said. "That dratted dragon."

"What do you mean?" Floyd asked looking but not seeing anything. Not even the edge of the tray because Gertrude covered it so completely.

"Gertrude's pinched the tray."

"You're a nutcase," said Floyd not knowing what else to say. After all the tray had disappeared.

"Watch out," said Nellie pushing Floyd out of the way and landing in a heap on top of him.

"Nellie," he shouted. "Why did you have to do that?"

"She tried to run us over," said Nellie clambering up.

Gertrude came to a bumpy halt. "It's great," she shouted. "I'm going to do it again."

"You've bent the tray," shouted Nellie.

"Not very much," said Gertrude and flew back up the hill.

"What do you mean, 'You've bent the tray'? Where *is* the tray?" Floyd asked.

"Watch out," Nellie said pushing Floyd out of the way again.

"That's not funny," Floyd said. He was getting fed up. He wanted his tray back.

"Give it back, Gertrude," said Nellie.

"You can have it," said Gertrude. She threw the tray across the snow and it landed near Floyd.

"I've found it," Floyd cried. He picked it up. They looked at it. It was bent and buckled to the shape of half of Gertrude's bottom. Neither of them would be able to sit on it now.

"How did that happen?" Floyd said. "You must have hit a bump."

Nellie didn't say anything. She was so cross. She could see Gertrude doing her exercises on the top of the hill. She hoped she would stay away from them for the rest of the morning.

"Let's make a snowman," she suggested. "It can have the tray for a hat. It's almost the right shape."

Floyd liked the idea and the two of them began rolling a giant snowball for the body. As soon as they began their snowman they noticed other children doing the same.

"Our park is going to have lots of snowmen," Nellie said.

"We could make them in a big circle," Floyd suggested.

"That's a good idea," Nellie agreed.

Floyd went and asked the other children if they would like to make a circle of snowmen. Some of them thought they would. Soon five snowmen were being built facing into a circle. The children patted and moulded the snow into arms and heads. They made buttons and eyes from stones they found in the snow holes Meg had dug. Pieces of twig made mouths and noses.

Nellie and Floyd put the tin tray on the head of their snowman. One had a scarf around his neck, another a pom pom hat on his head. They looked fine. The children were pleased. They left the snowmen and wandered off to play hide and seek.

Gertrude was doing running exercises. She saw the snowmen from the top of the hill. She trotted and slithered down to them, puffing, her hot breath making clouds of steam.

"What on earth are they? Sort of snow people." She did running on the spot. "I could do my deep breathing exercises with these," she said. "After all, they can't want them any more."

She stood in the middle of the circle and took a deep breath in through her nostrils and out again. Jets of steam blew around one of the snowmen. It began to melt. Gertrude turned to the next snowman and blew. Then the next and the next. Soon all the snowmen were running with water.

Nellie discovered her. She beat her fists against Gertrude's scaly body.

"You beast, you beast, you've melted our snowmen," she cried.

Gertrude wriggled and pushed Nellie away. "Oh, don't," she said. "That tickles."

"How *could* you?" Nellie said.

"I thought you had finished with them."

"There's no snow left to make any more!" Nellie cried.

Gertrude looked about her. There was a criss cross of green lines where the giant snowballs had been rolled. Nearly all the snow had gone showing the grass underneath.

"Sorry," she said. "I'll mend them for you, really I will."

"Where will you find any snow?"

"Leave that to me," said Gertrude. "I'm going to get a lot more exercise. Goody, goody."

She flew into the air with a great flapping of wings. She went very high and landed on top of a snow covered tree. She jumped from branch to branch pushing and pulling and shaking. Snow cascaded to the ground.

Nellie cheered up at once. She rushed to the bottom of the tree and carried armful after armful of fresh snow to the circle of snowmen. Gertrude arrived panting.

"I'll help," she said.

By the time Floyd came over, all the snowmen looked as good as new. "I think it's time to go home," he said. "My hands and feet are freezing. We can come and see our snowmen tomorrow."

Gertrude, who was feeling in a good mood, nearly blew hot air at Floyd but remembered in time not to. She didn't want to do any more melting.

When they got home Nellie said goodbye to Floyd on the front doorstep.

"It was a great morning," he said.

"It was," Nellie agreed.

Nellie and Meg went through their house to the kitchen. Making sure that Granny May wasn't watching, Nellie took a whole packet of chocolate biscuits from the biscuit tin. She and Meg took it to the old garden shed.

"This is for you," she said to Gertrude who was lying across her pile of sacks resting.

"Thank you, Nellie," Gertrude said. "No hard feelings?" Nellie grinned and shook her head. They left Gertrude munching the biscuits. The pair of them ran down the garden and back into the warmth of the house.

6

HEGGERTY HAGGERTY
and the
FLYING SAUCER

Elizabeth Lindsay

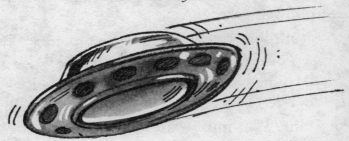

It all started one snowy winter's afternoon.
Heggerty Haggerty, Broomstick and Blackcat
had stayed indoors all day. It was beginning
to get dark and still the snowflakes were
falling.

Broomstick wanted to go outside. "Can't I
go out just for a little bit, please?" he asked.
Heggerty Haggerty shook her head.

"No you can't. Not while it's snowing like
this. You must wait until it's stopped."

"But I want to do something now,"
Broomstick said.

Heggerty Haggerty went to the bookshelf
and fetched a large green story book. "Why
don't you read this?" she said.

Broomstick took the book and sat at the
table. The title was *Imp and the Flying Saucer*.
Broomstick started reading straight away. He
read the book from beginning to end without
stopping.

"Did you enjoy it?" Heggerty Haggerty asked.

"I did," replied Broomstick, "because I like stories about flying saucers, and Imp had a great adventure with his."

Broomstick sat deep in thought. The one thing he wanted more than anything else in the world was his own flying saucer. He stared at the dresser. There were saucers all along the top shelf. The green one in the middle seemed to be winking at him. Broomstick had an idea.

"I could make my own flying saucer out of the green saucer using a special magic recipe."

Broomstick looked round. Heggerty Haggerty was busy in the kitchen. Blackcat was fast asleep in front of the fire. He fetched the *Book of Spells* and put it on the table. The green saucer on the dresser kept on winking. The *Book of Spells* seemed to know what Broomstick was looking for because it opened at a recipe which said:

"Saucer — magic flying. Recipe for.
Take one green saucer. Rub all over with two teaspoonfuls of moondust. Make following signs over saucer with fingers. Tap the saucer three times.

Say these words:

SAUCER GREEN SAUCER
VERY VERY SOON
YOU WILL BE MAGIC
AND CAN FLY TO THE MOON

Stand well back."

He remembered the recipe from beginning to end and closed the book with a thump.

Blackcat opened an eye and watched as Broomstick flew to the dresser to fetch the winking green saucer from the top shelf, and whisked upstairs with it. Blackcat wondered what Broomstick was up to.

Heggerty Haggerty carried a tray through from the kitchen.

"Supper's ready, Broomstick," she called.

After supper, Broomstick collected all the dishes and put them on the tray.

"I'll do the washing-up," he said. "All by myself."

"Thank you, Broomstick," said Heggerty Haggerty.

Broomstick carried the tray into the kitchen. He found a paper-bag and a teaspoon and carefully measured two teaspoonfuls of moondust into the paper-bag. Then he began the washing-up.

When the kitchen was quite tidy again Broomstick picked up the paper-bag and went into the living-room. He yawned the most enormous yawn.

"Goodness you seem tired," said Heggerty Haggerty.

Broomstick nodded. "I'll go up now. Night, night."

Blackcat stared suspiciously at the paper-bag Broomstick was holding behind his back.

"Goodnight, sleep tight," called Heggerty Haggerty as Broomstick flew upstairs.

Blackcat was very curious. He trotted upstairs after Broomstick. He peeped round Broomstick's bedroom door. Broomstick was sitting in the middle of the floor rubbing some sort of dust all over Heggerty Haggerty's green saucer. Then he made signs over it with his fingers.

Broomstick tapped the saucer three times and said:

"SAUCER GREEN SAUCER
VERY VERY SOON
YOU WILL BE MAGIC
AND CAN FLY TO THE MOON."

He stood against the wall.

The saucer began to glow a pale luminous green. A strange whirring noise began to fill the room as slowly the saucer grew. Soon it was as big as a plate, then as big as a table.

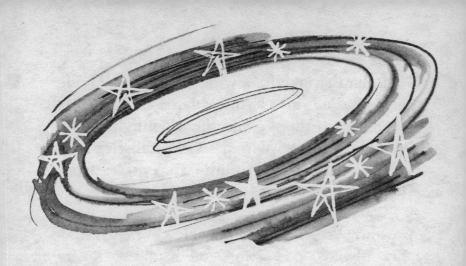

There was a green flash and the whirring noise stopped. Broomstick looked delighted.

"It's just like Imp's flying saucer," he said. "It's got a lid that lifts up, and inside are all the controls for flying it. It's perfect."

Blackcat's whiskers twitched. He stepped forward for a closer look.

"Hello, Blackcat," said Broomstick. "Do you want to come for a ride with me?"

Before Blackcat had a chance to say anything Broomstick lifted the dome and dropped Blackcat inside. He opened the bedroom window and climbed into the flying saucer himself. He closed the lid and pressed the GO button. With a whirr the saucer took off and flew out of the window.

It had stopped snowing. The countryside lay covered in a white blanket. The stars twinkled in the sky and the moonlight shone silver on to the whiteness. Broomstick and Blackcat stared down at the wintry scene from their flying saucer.

"This is the way to travel," cried Broomstick. "Let's visit the stars, Blackcat."

Broomstick pulled a lever and the green saucer sped into the sky leaving the snowy scene behind. Higher and higher it went until it seemed to have become a star itself.

Back indoors Heggerty Haggerty was beginning to feel a little chilly. She shivered.

"That's funny," she said. "I'm not imagining it. There is a draught. Now where's it coming from?"

Heggerty Haggerty looked at the hearthrug. No Blackcat.

"And where's Blackcat got to?" she wondered.

The draught seemed to be coming from upstairs. It was freezing on the landing. An icy breeze was rushing round Broomstick's half-opened door. Heggerty Haggerty went into the empty bedroom and found the window open.

"Whatever's going on?" she asked. "They can't have gone flying on a night like this. Unless . . . " Heggerty Haggerty had a thought. She went downstairs.

She noticed at once that the green saucer was missing from the dresser. She fetched the *Book of Spells* from behind the grandfather clock.

"Last recipe done, please," she said. The book opened at "Saucer — magic flying".

"I might have guessed," she said. "They could be halfway to the moon for all I know. I'd better think of something quickly."

Heggerty Haggerty looked around the room.

"I'll need a flying machine," she said. "And something to keep me warm."

She went into the kitchen and fetched the kettle. She thought she could make herself quite comfortable on that. She found a quick flying recipe in her *Book of Spells*. It was an easy one as it was made with finger clicks. They only took a second. Click, click, she went and the kettle grew. The handle made a very nice seat and steam came out of the spout.

"It'll keep my feet as warm as toast," she declared.

Heggerty Haggerty wrapped herself up warmly and put the *Book of Spells* in her pocket. She opened the front door and the kettle glided outside followed by Heggerty Haggerty.

"Goodness, it's chilly," she said and sat quickly on the kettle to get warmed up.

The kettle took off. As it happened the flying saucer was not all that far away. Broomstick had changed his mind about going as high as the stars and had turned the flying saucer earthwards. It whizzed across

the night sky flashing brightly. It was very exciting. Broomstick decided to land on the village green.

Constable Short was sitting in his police car outside the village shop. He looked up as the saucer went flying past. He couldn't believe his eyes.

"It's not. It can't be. It is," he gasped. And he yelled into his radio, "There's a flying saucer over the village. Send help at once."

Constable Short waited breathlessly, little knowing that Heggerty Haggerty was on the way. The kettle was very slow but at least it was getting her there and her feet were as warm as toast. She was surprised to find that she was enjoying herself, and was relieved to notice the flying saucer whizz across the sky above her.

As Heggerty Haggerty's kettle steamed into the village she could hear the sound of fire-engine sirens. She waved at Constable Short. He looked shocked to see her on the kettle.

"Where's Broomstick then?" he asked.

"In the flying saucer," said Heggerty Haggerty pointing upwards.

Constable Short started talking into his radio again. He looked embarrassed. He was even more embarrassed when the fire-engines arrived.

"False alarm," he said to the firemen.

"What's that then?" said the chief fireman pointing to the flying saucer which was coming in to land. The firemen pointed their hoses at the green saucer.

Heggerty Haggerty unmagic-ed the flying saucer with the words:

"FLYING GREEN SAUCER LISTEN TO ME
SAUCEROUS SOCK TIC AT ONCE."

There was a whirring noise as the flying saucer became the green saucer from the dresser again.

"Oh!" said the firemen, surprised. They put away their hoses and drove their engines home. Constable Short waved as Heggerty Haggerty, Broomstick and Blackcat steamed past on the kettle.

At home Heggerty Haggerty unmagic-ed the kettle and put the green saucer back on the dresser.

She tucked Broomstick up in bed and settled herself down with a nice cup of cocoa.

Blackcat curled up on her lap and went to sleep.

JUGGLERS

There are books to suit everyone in Hippo's JUGGLERS series:

When I Lived Down Cuckoo Lane
by Jean Wills   £1.75
A small girl and her family move into a new house in Cuckoo Lane. Follow her adventures through the year as she makes friends, starts a new school, learns to ride a bike, and even helps out at her father's shop.

The Secret of Bone Island by Sam McBratney   £1.75
Linda, Peter and Gareth are very curious about Bone Island. Especially when they're told some weird stories about the island's history. And then three suspicious-looking men warn them to stay away from the island . . .

Stan's Galactic Bug by John Emlyn Edwards   £1.75
Stan can't believe his eyes when his computer game traps an alien from outer space. It's up to Stan to save the intergalactic traveller from destruction!

As If By Magic by Jo Furminger   £1.75
Natasha has never seen a girl as weird as Harriet – the new girl in the class. But not only does she *look* strange, with her dark tatty clothes and bright green eyes, but the oddest things start to happen when she's around.

Look out for these other titles in the JUGGLERS series:

Bags of Trouble by Michael Harrison
The Jiggery-Pokery Cup by Angela Bull

STREAMERS

We've got lots of great books for younger readers in Hippo's STREAMERS series:

Sally Ann – On Her Own by Terrance Dicks   £1.75
Sally Ann is a very special toy. She's a rag doll who likes to be involved in everything that's going on. When Sally Ann finds out that the nursery school where she lives might be closed down, she decides it's time to take action!

Sally Ann – The School Play by Terrance Dicks £1.75
When the nursery school's electricity goes off, Sally Ann comes up with a wonderful idea to pay for the new wiring. But not everything runs as smoothly as Sally Ann would like!

The Little Yellow Taxi and His Friends
by Ruth Ainsworth   £1.75
The little grey car can't get to sleep at night, and keeps all the other cars and lorries awake. So the garage owner paints the little car yellow, gives him a sign for his roof, and turns him into an all-night taxi.

Tom by Ruth Silvestre   £1.75
The circus has come to town, and Tom tries to tell his parents about it. But they are always too busy to listen. . . A delightful collection of stories about Tom, his family and friends.

Look out for these other titles in the STREAMERS series:

Nate the Great by Marjorie Sharmat
Nate the Great and the Missing Key by Marjorie Sharmat

HIPPO BOOKS FOR YOUNGER READERS

If you've enjoyed this book, you'll probably be interested to know that there are loads more Hippo books to suit all kinds of tastes. You'll find scary spooky books, gripping adventure stories, funny books, and lots lots more.

You'll find these and many more fun Hippo books at your local bookshop, or you can order them direct. Just send off to *Customer Services, Hippo Books, Westfield Road, Southam, Leamington Spa, Warwickshire CV33 0JH*, not forgetting to enclose a cheque or postal order for the price of the book(s) plus 30p per book for postage and packing.